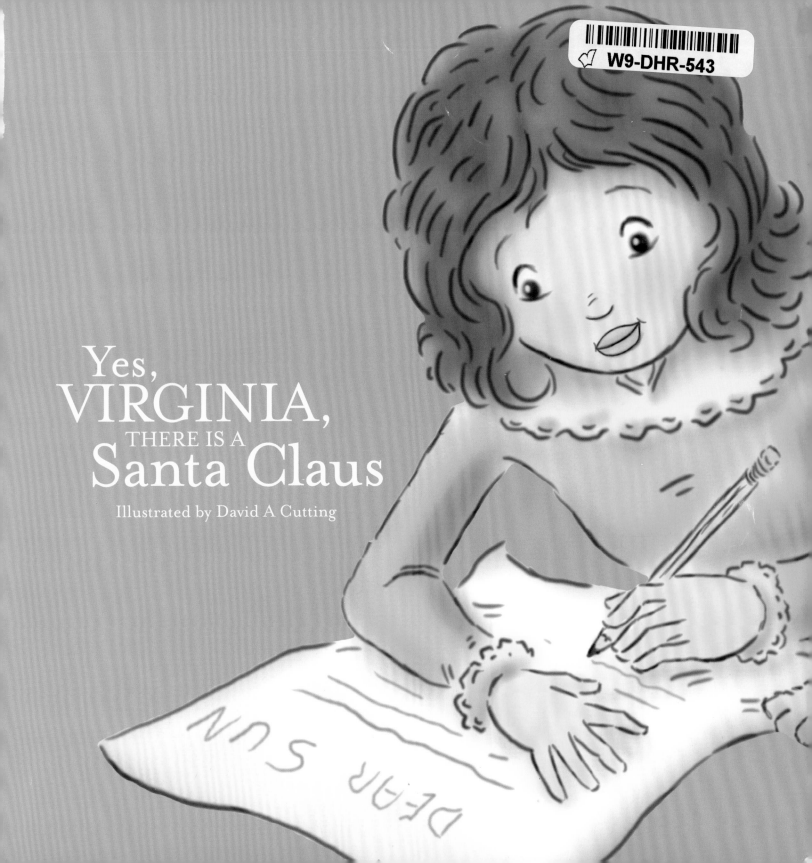

Yes, VIRGINIA, THERE IS A Santa Claus

Illustrated by David A Cutting

I want to tell you a true story. This story happened a long time ago. This story happened more than one hundred years ago. It is about a little girl named Virginia O'Hanlon.

One day in 1897, when Virginia was eight years old, she asked her dad about Santa Claus. She wanted to know if he was real. She had begun to doubt Santa Claus, because her friends had told her that Santa did not exist.

Virginia's dad was named Dr. Philip O'Hanlon.
Dr. O'Hanlon knew that Santa Claus was real
but wanted to reassure Virginia, so he suggested
she write to the newspaper and ask them the same
question. Virginia lived in New York City.
At that time in New York City, there was a
newspaper known as *The Sun*, and it was very
popular. So she decided to write *The Sun* a letter.

When *The Sun* received the letter, it was given to a man named Francis P. Church so that he may answer Virginia.

Virginia's letter and Mr. Church's response were both printed in the newspaper. These two letters were so special and so meaningful that people still read them and know about them to this day.

Here is *exactly* what they said…

Is There a Santa Claus?

We take pleasure in answering at once and thus prominently the communication below, expressing at the same time our great gratification that its faithful author is numbered among the friends of THE SUN:

"DEAR EDITOR:
I am 8 years old.
"Some of my little friends say there is no Santa Claus.
"Papa says, 'If you see it in THE SUN it's so.'
"Please tell me the truth; is there a Santa Claus?"

VIRGINIA O'HANLON

"VIRGINIA, your little friends are wrong. They have been affected by the skepticism of a skeptical age. They do not believe except [what] they see. They think that nothing can be which is not comprehensible by their little minds."

"All minds, VIRGINIA, whether they be men's or children's, are little. In this great universe of ours, man is a mere insect, an ant, in his intellect, as compared with the boundless world about him, as measured by the intelligence capable of grasping the whole of truth and knowledge.

"Yes, VIRGINIA, there is a Santa Claus. He exists as certainly as love and generosity and devotion exist, and you know that they abound and give to your life its highest beauty and joy.

"Alas! How dreary would be the world if there were no Santa Claus. It would be as dreary as if there were no VIRGINIAS. There would be no childlike faith then, no poetry, no romance to make tolerable this existence. We should have no enjoyment, except in sense and sight. The eternal light with which childhood fills the world would be extinguished."

"Not believe in Santa Claus! You might as well not believe in fairies!
You might get your papa to hire men to watch in all the chimneys on
Christmas Eve to catch Santa Claus, but even if they did not see
Santa Claus coming down,what would that prove?

"Nobody sees Santa Claus, but that is no sign that there is no
Santa Claus. The most real things in the world are those that
neither children nor men can see. Did you ever see fairies
dancing on the lawn? Of course not, but that's no
proof that they are not there. Nobody can conceive
or imagine all the wonders there are unseen and
unseeable in the world."

"You may tear apart the baby's rattle and see what makes the noise inside, but there is a veil covering the unseen world which not the strongest man, nor even the united strength of all the strongest men that ever lived, could tear apart. Only faith, fancy, poetry, love, romance, can push aside that curtain and view and picture the supernal beauty and glory beyond it. Is it all real? Ah, VIRGINIA, in all this world there is nothing else real and abiding."

"No Santa Claus! Thank God he lives, and he lives forever. A thousand years from now, VIRGINIA, nay, ten times ten thousand years from now, he will continue to make glad the heart of childhood."

So now you know Virginia's story. I hope you liked the letter from Mr. Church at the newspaper.

I loved it. And I know Virginia loved it, too.

THE END.